A Tree in a Forest

BY JAN THORNHILL

SIMON & SCHUSTER BOOKS FOR YOUNG READERS
Published by Simon & Schuster
New York · London · Toronto · Sydney · Tokyo · Singapore

SIMON & SCHUSTER BOOKS FOR YOUNG READERS
Simon & Schuster Building, Rockefeller Center
1230 Avenue of the Americas, New York, New York 10020
Copyright © 1991 by Jan Thornhill
First U.S. edition 1992
All rights reserved including the right of reproduction
in whole or in part in any form.
First published in Canada by Greey de Pencier Books in 1991
SIMON & SCHUSTER BOOKS FOR YOUNG READERS
is a trademark of Simon & Schuster.
Manufactured in Hong Kong

10 9 8 7 6 5 4 3 2 1

Library of Congress Cataloging-in-Publication Data
Thornhill, Jan. A tree in a forest / written and illustrated
by Jan Thornhill. p. cm. Summary: Presents the life story
of a 200-year-old maple tree.
1. Forest ecology—Juvenile literature. 2. Maple—Ecology—
Juvenile literature. [1. Maple. 2. Trees. 3. Forest ecology.
4. Ecology.] I. Title. QH541.5.F6T53 1992
574.5′2642—dc20 91-25857 CIP ISBN: 0-671-75901-9

A Tree in a Forest

EVERY FOREST is an amazing community of living things—of green plants and brilliant mushrooms, of nibbling deer and darting birds, of insects and spiders and tiny bacteria. Each animal and plant relies in its own special way on the trees of the forest.

Trees are the biggest plants on Earth. Their long winding roots help to hold fertile soil to the ground. Their leaves clean and enrich the air. They nourish and shelter and protect all kinds of other living things.

From the instant its life begins, every tree in every forest has its own special story to tell. This is one story—the story of a maple tree. Its life begins more than two hundred years ago, long before your great-great-great-grandparents were even born.

IT IS EARLY MORNING in a maple forest, long, long ago.
Under the pale rays of the rising sun, a redstart awakens, shakes its feathers,
and begins to sing.

Summer

A soft breeze tickles its way between the trees. Leaves flutter. Clusters of dangling maple keys quiver and dance, the seeds they hold slowly ripening in the warmth of the summer sun.

Summer

ON A BLUSTERY AUTUMN afternoon, noisy crows caw to one another as they begin their long journey south. On the ground, squirrels bustle about, gathering nuts and seeds. One cracks open a beechnut to get at its meat, while another busily buries a cache of seeds that it will feast on during the cold winter months to come.

With each gust of wind the air swirls with falling maple keys, each one holding a tiny ripe seed within its papery husk. The wind catches the keys by their curved flat wings, sending them dizzily spinning to the forest floor.

Chipmunks, squirrels and mice snatch up the maple keys, eating a few immediately but storing many more for winter. Tiny insects burrow into other keys, nibbling away at their precious contents until all that is left of each is a hollowed-out shell.

One maple key twirls down from a high branch and lands on an old log. A moment later, a big leaf wafts down and covers the key, hiding it from the hungry eyes of forest creatures.

THROUGHOUT THE LONG winter, the maple key on the log lies beneath a thick blanket of snow. By late winter the snow is very deep. Deer and rabbits chew on tender young saplings, the only food they can find. Hungry squirrels dig everywhere, hoping to uncover the last of their buried seeds.

As the days grow longer, the sun begins to warm the leafless forest. For weeks the air is filled with the trickling and dripping sounds of melting ice and snow. Then one day, there are suddenly other sounds in the forest: the singing and twittering of birds returning to their nesting grounds.

Winter

THE SMELL OF WET EARTH mingles with the scent of hundreds of woodland flowers. Surrounded by the soft new leaves of a young maple, a pair of warblers work on their nest. A mother wolf brings her cubs out of their winter den for their first romp and tumble in the fresh spring air.

On the old log, the life of a new maple tree begins. The seed inside the maple key swells with moisture until its seed coat splits apart. A tiny root creeps down into the damp, rotted wood of the old log. In the warm weeks that follow, the maple seedling stretches its first leaves to the sun.

Spring

EARLY ONE SUMMER, the maple seedling on the log droops from thirst. For a whole month no rain has fallen, not a single drop. The forest floor is so dry that robins can easily hear earthworms moving about beneath the crisp fallen leaves. Every living thing is thirsty. Leaves wilt, animals pant.

During the drought, many maple seedlings shrivel and die. Their young roots are too short to reach water deep in the soil. The little maple is still alive because the rotted log holds water like a sponge. But now even the log is beginning to dry out.

At last huge storm clouds darken the sky. Thunder grumbles through the forest. But before the rain begins to fall, a brilliant bolt of lightning slashes into a dead tree. Orange flames sweep down its trunk until they lick the dry forest floor. In an instant the flames are darting along the ground, burning up everything in their path. Terrified birds and animals flee for their lives.

As the fire races closer and closer to the tiny maple on the log, the first few drops of rain spatter down from the sky. Through black, billowing clouds of smoke, the rain begins to fall in sheets. Pelting down harder and harder, it smothers the flames before they can reach the tiny tree.

DURING THE SPRING and summer, the leaves of the tree are green because they are full of chlorophyll, a green substance that helps the tree make food for itself.

In the autumn, the tree prepares for a long sleep. When the first cold nights dust the forest with frost, the chlorophyll in the leaves begins to disintegrate and food-making stops. As the green chlorophyll gradually disappears, other colors that have been hiding in each leaf all along suddenly appear. Almost overnight, the tree's leaves turn from green to yellow, from yellow to brilliant orange, from orange to burning red. One by one, the bright leaves flutter to the forest floor.

AS THE DAYS GROW COLDER and the ground begins to freeze, the tree's roots stop drinking. The watery sap that carries food throughout the tree moves more and more slowly until finally one day it stops. By the time the first snow flies, the tree is asleep.

Many forest animals go to sleep too. They hibernate for the months when they will not be able to find enough food to eat. A chipmunk, rolled into a furry ball, sleeps underground, sheltered by the tree's roots. Inside the rotted log a tangle of snakes lies coiled together, while in the hollow base of a nearby tree a family of skunks curls up in a warm bundle, sleeping through the bone-chilling cold and howling blizzards of winter.

25 years old

ON A HOT MIDSUMMER afternoon, four hungry young cuckoos loudly greet their mother when she returns to the nest. In her beak she holds a hairy caterpillar, the nestlings' favorite food. On another branch of the tree, a fat cicada bug trills in the heat of the day.

The whole forest buzzes and hums. Bees and butterflies sip sweet nectar from flower blossoms. Ladybugs, praying mantises and walkingsticks look for smaller insects to eat. Caterpillars nibble on living green leaves, while other insects eat dead leaves and rotting branches that have fallen to the ground.

At night, bats swoop between the trees, snapping up mosquitoes and other flying insects. Redstarts and flycatchers flit through the forest, hunting the same insects during the day. Bears eat mouthfuls of ants or bees and lick into beehives to get at the sweet honey inside. Skunks dig june bug larvae from the ground and root around in logs looking for fat beetle grubs.

Most insects will freeze when autumn chills the forest. Many of the birds who eat these insects will fly south for the winter to warmer places where insects abound all year long.

ONE WINTER NIGHT a silvery rain falls on the forest. The air is so cold that as each drop lands it freezes instantly. Before long, every branch of every tree is coated with glimmering, crystal-clear ice. The snow on the ground is covered with ice too, ice thick enough to skate on.

As the sun rises, the clouds break apart and the rain stops. The forest sparkles as if it is crusted with diamonds. Every now and then, when a breeze comes along, the air is filled with the delicate, tinkling sound of falling ice.

The shining ice is very heavy on the maple's branches. Under the unbearable weight, one big branch snaps. The sharp sound cracks through the still forest, startling a group of chickadees into flight.

The ice covering the snow is so hard that some hungry animals can't get to their food. It would take days for a squirrel to dig through with its tiny claws to get at a buried cache of seeds. Not even a wolf can break the ice. It can only cock its head and lick its lips while it listens to the sound of mice skittering to and fro beneath its feet.

IN VERY EARLY SPRING, when the days have grown warm and sunny, but the nights are still frosty, the sap in the maple tree suddenly begins to flow again.

The native people knew how to make a delicious syrup by boiling down the sweet sap of sugar maples. When early settlers arrived, the native people taught them how to tap the trees and gather the sap. While two pileated woodpeckers glide from tree to tree, searching for a hole to nest in, a farm family is hard at work "sugaring off," making maple syrup and maple sugar that they will use all year long. The farmer taps one last tree by drilling a hole in its trunk. He will fit a spout into the hole, then hang a bucket from the spout.

100 years old

Every day for almost two weeks sap leaks from the trees, drop by drop, filling the buckets over and over again. As the buckets fill, the family collects the watery sap and pours it into huge iron pots hung over hot fires. The boiling sap bubbles and foams, steam rising from it in puffy white clouds. With each passing hour the sap grows sweeter, until finally it thickens into syrup. So much water must boil away that it takes almost forty buckets of sap to make just one bucket of syrup. When the syrup is boiled even longer, it hardens into maple sugar.

FOR THE FIFTH TIME this late spring day, a hawk carries food to her nest in the highest branches of the tree. Her two chicks greedily eye the snake she has brought them. On another branch, a redstart sits on her clutch of eggs. Where the branch broke off in the ice storm, a hole has grown in the trunk of the tree, home now to a family of downy woodpeckers. On the ground far below, a skunk parades along with her kits.

Each spring, while birds and animals are busy taking care of their young, the maple tree is busy producing young of its own. Clusters of delicate flowers dangle between the tree's new leaves.

125 years old

BEES AND OTHER INSECTS buzz and hover from one flower to the next. As they collect sweet nectar with their mouthparts, powdery pollen clings to tiny hairs on their legs and bodies. Flying from blossom to blossom, the insects fertilize the flowers by carrying pollen from male flower parts to female flower parts. Fertilized flowers become the tree's fruit, the keys that hold the maple's seeds.

Each spring the tree grows flowers, and the flowers, fertilized by insects or the wind, grow into maple keys. And each spring, animals and birds raise their young in the tree. As time passes, the rotted-out hole grows large enough to shelter a family of raccoons and, higher up, owls rebuild the hawk's nest.

150 years old

ON A STEAMY SUMMER afternoon, silence cloaks the maple forest. No squirrels chatter, no birds sing. The air is completely still. The only sound is the occasional trilling of a cicada bug high in a tree. As blue-black storm clouds swell on the horizon, deep rumblings of faraway thunder roll toward the forest.

Within minutes, the massive clouds have completely blocked the sun. The forest is dark and hushed, waiting. In an instant, the wind is upon it, a violent wind that makes the highest branches of the tallest trees thrash and flail against one another. Flashes of lightning illuminate the clouds, thunder shakes the earth. Driven by the wind, rain pelts down as hard as hail.

Suddenly, a huge bolt of lightning streaks down from the clouds. There is a terrifying crack as it strikes the tree. With a sickening, splitting noise, the top of the tree breaks apart from the trunk and crashes to the ground.

THE CLEAR BLUE LIGHT of a full moon falls on the maple forest. A small pack of wolves has gathered. They sniff at one another, leave signs for other wolves, and howl, noses pointed to the starry night sky. Another hunter, the great horned owl, sails by on broad, silent wings. It turns its head first one way, then the other. Its sharp eyes slide over the forest, searching for a sleeping bird or the movement of a deer mouse scurrying across the snow.

A flying squirrel glides silently through the air. The only sound it makes is a tiny *tick* when it lands on the trunk of the tree.

195 years old

The tree has been alive for nearly two hundred years. This is a very long time, even for a maple tree.

High up, a large hole has grown where the tree was struck by lightning. The hole will make it hard for sap to flow freely in the spring. But the tree is still strong. Enough sap will flow through its remaining branches to feed the growth of new green leaves when winter is gone.

195 years old

THIS SPRING THE HOLES in the tree have grown much bigger. Very little sap has risen to feed new growth, but there are still a few healthy branches covered with leaves. The tips of some of the highest branches are bare. These branches have been harmed by acid rain caused by air pollution. Even young, healthy trees can be poisoned by acid rain.

There are so many holes in the tree now that dozens of animals and birds have made it their home. A family of flying squirrels uses one hole. In another, three young pileated woodpeckers, almost old enough to fly from the nest, open their beaks wide when their father returns with a mouthful of insects to eat.

The frail old tree provides food for all kinds of forest creatures. A porcupine gnaws bark off a branch with its sharp yellow teeth, leaving the wood beneath naked and bright. Woodpeckers whack their beaks, *rat-a-tat-tat*, over and over again into the tree's trunk, knocking off bits of bark to get at insects and larvae tunneling through the wood beneath.

Nearer the ground, honey mushrooms and shelf fungi get food from the tree in their own way, digesting parts of it with threadlike strands. And millions of bacteria, invisible to the naked eye, are busy at work breaking down dead wood.

A BITING FALL WIND plucks leaves from the forest floor, whirls them up and spins them around, then drops them to the ground again. Two blue jays fly from one tree to the next, piping and quarreling, while a downy woodpecker pecks out one last insect before the sun goes down.

The tree's old trunk is rotted out and full of holes. No new wood has grown for four years now. This autumn the wind is stronger than the tree. It surges in through the holes, then rushes out again. It swirls powerfully around the trunk and with one mighty gust, wrenches the tree from its roots. Slowly, the tree falls. A family of deer mice leaps to safety as brittle branches snap and bark falls off in sheets. With a sorrowful sound, the huge old tree crashes to the forest floor.

Fall

CHIPMUNKS AND SNAKES, salamanders and toads, rabbits and spiders all seek shelter in the hollow trunk of the fallen tree. A skunk claws at the rotting log and roots around in its softening wood to get at the insects it likes to eat.

Bit by bit, year by year, the tree crumbles and decays. Tunneling insects grind its wood and bark into sawdust that other insects, in turn, will eat. Fungi and tiny bacteria break down what remains into rich forest soil. As the maple tree slowly decomposes, its substance returns to the earth.

Summer

ONE SPRING A MAPLE SEED takes root in the rich, rotting wood of the
big old log. By the time the trilliums and trout lilies are in bloom, a tiny maple
seedling is stretching its new green leaves to the sun.

Spring

Another life, and another story, has begun.

Spring

THAT NEW LIFE will be recorded in the new tree's trunk, just as the life of the old tree can be counted in the rings in its thick trunk—one formed for each of its 212 years.

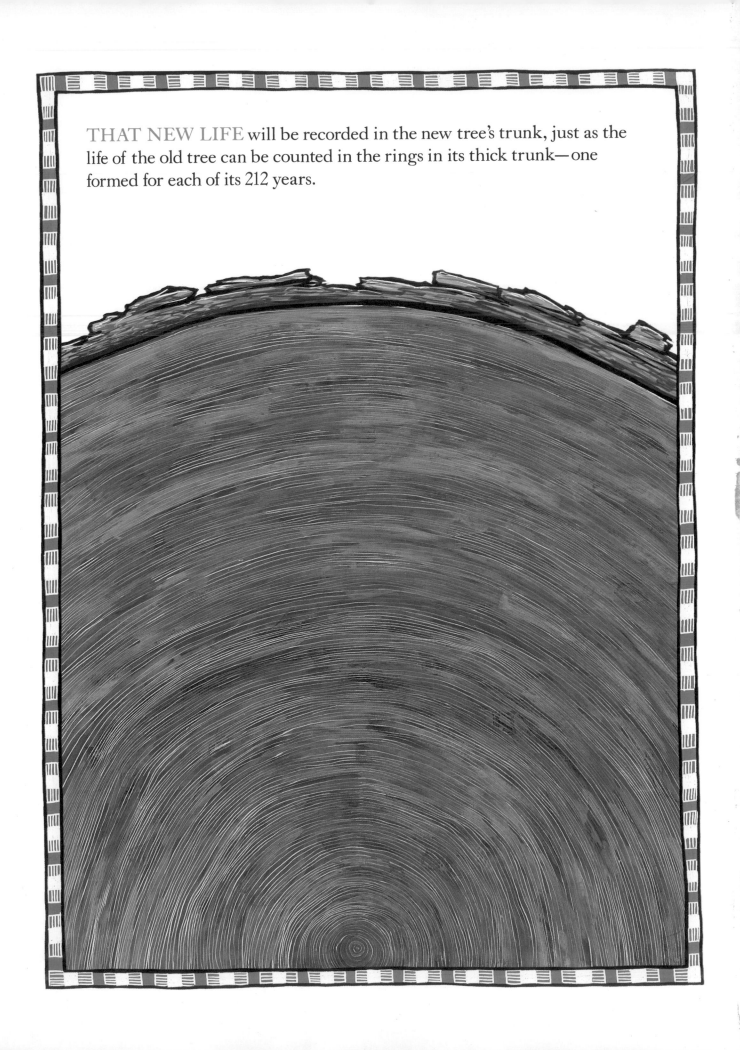